MATT PHELAN

PIGNIC

GREENWILLOW BOOKS, *An Imprint of* HarperCollins*Publishers*

Library of Congress Cataloging-in-Publication Data
Names: Phelan, Matt, author, illustrator.
Title: Pignic / written and illustrated by Matt Phelan.
Description: First edition. | New York, NY : Greenwillow Books, an imprint of
    HarperCollinsPublishers, [2018] | Summary: "A pig experiences adversity
    but in the end enjoys a perfect summer day"—Provided by publisher.
Identifiers: LCCN 2016050279 | ISBN 9780062443397 (hardcover)
Subjects: | CYAC: Pigs—Fiction. | Play—Fiction. | Summer—Fiction.
Classification: LCC PZ7.P44882 Pi 2018 | DDC [E]—dc23 LC record available at https://lccn.loc.gov/2016050279
18 19 20 21 22 SCP 10 9 8 7 6 5 4 3 2 1
First Edition

Greenwillow Books

For Jasper

It's a perfect day for a pignic.

There is a tree to climb!

Uh-oh.

Too high.

HOORAY!

There is a kite to fly!

Uh-oh.

No wind.

HOORAY!

Pretzels! Pies! Pickles!
And plums!

Uh-oh.

Dark clouds.

Mud?

Mud!

What a perfect day for a pignic.